MARY-KATE & ASHLEY

Starring in

SWITCHING GOALS

A novelization by Lisa Fiedler

Based on the teleplay by
David Kukoff & Matt Roshkow

A PARACHUTE PRESS BOOK

PARACHUTE
PRESS

Parachute Publishing, L.L.C
156 Fifth Avenue
Suite 302
New York, NY 10010

 DUALSTAR
PUBLICATIONS

Dualstar Publications
c/o Thorne and Company
A Professional Law Corporation
1801 Century Park East, Twelfth Floor
Los Angeles, CA 90067

Troll Communications L.L.C.
100 Corporate Drive
Mahwah, NJ 07430

ISBN 1-57351-005-X

First Printing: November 1999
Printed in the United States of America

10 9 8 7 6 5 4 3 2 1

CHAPTER ONE

"Perfect fit," said a voice behind Samantha Stanton.

Sam placed a new trophy on her shelf. She and her dad had won it that morning in the wheelbarrow race at the school carnival. She turned to see her twin sister, Emma, in the doorway.

Sam had to agree with Emma. The trophy *did* fit perfectly with all her other athletic awards.

Emma gave a big sigh and dropped down on her ruffly pink bed. She seemed very gloomy.

"Hey, it was just a goofy wheelbarrow race," Sam said quickly. "No big deal."

Emma looked at the tall, shiny new addition to Sam's collection. "Yeah, right."

"Okay," Sam admitted. "From here it looks good. But you should see it up close. That little gold lady on top has this miserable look on her face."

Emma managed a small smile.

"You don't have to say that, Sam," she said. "I know you're proud of all those awards. And you

1

should be. I'm proud of you for winning them. It's just that"—she picked up a hand mirror from her night table and gazed into it, frowning at her big blue eyes and shining blond hair—"I sometimes wonder if there's such a thing as an adopted twin."

"Nope. There isn't," Sam told her.

"Well, it sure feels like it sometimes." Emma sighed. "I mean, we look exactly alike. But when it comes to sports, it's like you and I are from different planets. How can I be so terrible at something you're so good at?"

Now it was Sam's turn to sigh. "Being a jock has its bad points, you know."

"What do you mean?" Emma asked.

"Well, for example there's the whole boy thing. I mean, I'd trade every one of those trophies for just one of the looks you get from the guys in school."

Emma sat up. "What are you talking about?" she asked. "Guys are always coming up to you."

"Yeah. To ask if they can borrow my hockey stick. Or if I'll be place-kicker for their football team!" Sam folded her arms. "Romantic, huh?"

Emma thought for a moment. Then she nodded. "Okay, I see your point. It's like they say: The grass is always greener..."

"...on a well-kept soccer field?" Sam teased.

"Well, I was going to say, when you're walking on it with a cute guy." Emma grinned.

Her grin slowly faded. "You know what the worst thing is? Sometimes, when you and Dad are doing sports, I think he forgets I'm alive."

"That's crazy." Sam sat beside her sister.

Every time Sam went from her side of the room to Emma's, she felt as if she were crossing into another dimension. Her twin's area was pastel and pretty. It was also as neat as a pin. Sam's own half looked like a locker room.

Occasionally, Emma would complain about Sam's mess. Or all her sports posters. And once in a while, Sam gave Emma a hard time about her frilly lampshade. Or her nine zillion bottles of nail polish. But overall, it was a good arrangement. The girls weren't just twins. They were best friends.

Sam had to make her sister feel better.

"Don't be so hard on yourself," she said. "I mean it, Em. You could be pretty good at sports yourself!"

"Hah! Then why didn't Dad pick *me* today?"

Sam thought back to that morning at the carnival. Everything had started off as usual. Sam devoured a corn dog while Emma flirted with a cute boy from their seventh-grade class. Of course, he asked Emma to ride the Ferris wheel with him. Sam passed the time with some cotton candy.

After that, Sam polished off a rainbow slushie. Then she watched as another cute guy threw softballs at milk bottles to win Emma a teddy bear. Then Sam threw her own softballs. She won a gigantic stuffed platypus. It could have swallowed Emma's bear in one gulp.

And then...their dad showed up.

"Okay, girls," he called, bounding toward them. "This is it!"

"What's up?" Sam asked.

Jerry Stanton grinned at his daughters. "It's time to show this crowd who the real champs are! Time to separate the men from the boys!"

Emma's eyes lit up. "Boys? Sounds like my kind of game!"

Sam laughed. Their father missed the joke.

"That's just an expression, Em. I'm talking about the big event...the wheelbarrow race!"

The twins exchanged glances. Their dad had been a sports star in high school and college. He was the owner of the biggest sporting goods store in town. For years, Jerry's Wide World of Sports had sponsored the only undefeated team in the Evansville Youth Soccer League. Jerry Stanton coached it, and he was tough. Winning was his life.

Jerry studied his daughters. "Let's see," he said. "Who's going to be my wheels?"

As if there were any doubt. Sam was always her father's choice for anything related to sports.

"Ready to bring home the gold, Sammy girl?"

"Sure!" Sam grinned. Then she caught the disappointed look on Emma's face. "I mean—"

"Great. Let's go!" Jerry took off at a jog toward the starting line.

Sam turned to Emma. "You'd hate being his wheelbarrow," she said. She gave her sister's shoulder a gentle punch. "It would ruin your manicure."

"Right," said Emma. She looked down at her polished nails.

Sam felt a twinge of guilt. But what could she do? The race was about to begin.

She hurried to the starting line, planted her palms in the dirt, and kicked up her heels for her father to catch. "Okay, Dad. We're going to win this one!"

Emma didn't feel like watching the race. Glumly, she headed over to the fortune telling booth. "Madam Denise," the fortune teller, was also known as Denise Stanton, PhD. And *also* known as Sam and Emma's mom.

5

A little boy plunked down a quarter to have his fortune told. Emma watched as her mom waved her hands over a crystal ball. The ball looked a lot like an upside-down fishbowl to Emma.

"Madam Denise" leaned close to the crystal ball. She narrowed her green eyes. "The spirits are responding," she said in a fake gypsy accent. "I see that you will face many challenges in your future."

She stopped and frowned. "That is not to say you should find those challenges daunting," she told the kid. Her voice had changed to its familiar, professional tone. "Self-doubt is perhaps the greatest block to personal success."

The kid just blinked at Madam Denise. Emma smiled and gave his shoulder a pat. "That's her way of saying hang tough," she explained. "Got it?"

The little boy stared for another second. Then he stuck his tongue out at Madam Denise and skipped off toward the Weight Guessing booth.

Madam Denise adjusted her turban. "Non-believers," she grumbled.

"Almost as bad as non-athletes," said Emma.

Her mother raised an eyebrow. "What's *that* supposed to mean?"

Before Emma could answer, she heard a roaring cheer. It was coming from the crowd at the finish line of the wheelbarrow race. She and her mother turned around.

A beaming Sam was being hoisted onto her father's shoulders. Someone was handing her an enormous trophy.

"Oh," Denise Stanton said gently. "I get it now."

The cheering faded. The judge's voice was booming through his bullhorn. "Continuing their father-daughter tradition in the wheelbarrow competition," he announced, "Jerry and Sam Stanton are our first place winners, three years running!"

"Yippee," Emma muttered.

Denise draped an arm around her. "You'd think they'd be bored with it by now," she said.

"Dad? Bored with winning?" Emma nodded toward the champions. "Does he look bored to you?"

"No," her mom admitted. She sighed.

Silently, Emma watched the celebration. Her dad was leading the crowd in a chant. *Sam-my, Sam-my, Sam-my...*

"Just once," Emma said softly, "I'd like to know how that feels."

CHAPTER TWO

After dinner, the girls went upstairs to finish their homework. Denise Stanton turned to her husband. "Jerry, we've got to talk."

"Uh-oh." Jerry put down the plate he was drying. "What did I do?"

Denise frowned. "It's not what you *did*. It's what you *didn't* do. You *didn't* ask Emma to be your partner in the wheelbarrow race."

"That's because I wanted to win," Jerry blurted out. Then he realized how bad that sounded.

His wife scowled at him. "You should have seen Emma's face. She was heartbroken."

"Oh." Jerry looked at the floor. A pang of guilt hit him. "I didn't mean to hurt her feelings."

"I know," Denise told him. "Your need to win got in the way of your judgement. But really, Jerry. Would it have been so bad to come in second place? If it meant giving Emma a chance?"

"*Second* place?" Jerry said with horror.

"There!" Denise cried. She threw up her hands.

"That's what I'm talking about! This was a junior high school wheelbarrow race, Jerry. Not the Olympics. But that's not even the point. It's the way you've labeled the girls. You see Sam as the jock, and Emma as the princess."

"Yes," Jerry agreed. "Because it's true!"

"But there's so much more to both of them! There's more to Sam than sports. There's more to Emma than cool clothes. Trust me." Denise was quiet for a moment. When she spoke again, her voice was serious. "The real problem is that you always leave Emma out. When you and Sam play catch in the backyard, Emma is left out. When you and Sam watch the Super Bowl, or the World Series, Emma is left out. And that hurts her."

Jerry shrugged. "Maybe if she cared a little more about sports…"

"Or maybe," Denise broke in, "if *you* cared a little less!"

Without another word, she turned and left the kitchen.

The next morning when Jerry Stanton arrived at work, his assistant, Dave, gave him the worst news of his life.

"Co-ed?" Jerry couldn't believe his ears. "Did you

say *co-ed*? As in, boys and girls *together*?"

Dave nodded. "That's what I said, boss. The youth soccer league…"

"Youth soccer league," Jerry repeated. He waved wildly toward a wall packed with framed photos and championship plaques. "The one in which I have sponsored and coached an all-boys team for the last six years. *That* youth soccer league?"

"Yes," Dave said. "*That* youth soccer league is now planning to include…"

Jerry closed his eyes tightly. "Girls."

Dave cleared his throat. "Uh, yeah. Girls."

Jerry opened his eyes again. He looked at the display of awards. They had all been earned by his team, the Hurricanes. He sank into a chair his customers used when they tried on sneakers.

"You know what this means? We won't just be dealing with torn ligaments and pulled muscles. We'll be dealing with…"

"…bad hair days," Dave finished.

Jerry nodded. "And don't even get me started on the 'these-shoes-don't-match-my-shin-guards' issue. This is a sad day for organized sports, Dave."

Dave nodded solemnly. "Yes, sir, it is."

Jerry slumped in his chair. He was already worried enough about the Hurricanes, ever since he'd gotten the news that his star forward, Tony Selby, had moved to Denver to live with his father.

And now this. He didn't need this.

Especially after what Denise said to him about Emma the night before. Jerry was worried about Emma. He knew he was going to have to find some way to bond with her. Not that he didn't want to. He just didn't know how.

He could rattle off the batting averages of every ballplayer in the major league. And Emma thought Joe DiMaggio was an Italian clothing designer. What did they have in common?

Jerry's eyes turned to a framed snapshot on the wall. It was a team photo after the first Hurricanes squad had won the championship. That was six years ago. Sitting cross-legged in front of the boys was his honorary team manager. A smiling, seven-year-old Sam. Even then she'd been as good as most of the players.

Hey. Co-ed soccer meant Sam could play on his team! She might just be his new forward....

Suddenly, Jerry felt a glimmer of hope. "Then again," he said, jumping up, "maybe this is the start of something wonderful!"

CHAPTER THREE

That evening, Sam tried to concentrate on her homework. It was hard, because her parents were talking in the hall.

Then she heard two words: "soccer" and "co-ed."

Those were words that could change a girl's life! Sam jumped up from her bed and dashed into the hall. She had to hurdle Emma, who was lying on the floor with the phone glued to her ear.

The hallway was empty. Sam's parents had gone into their bedroom.

Sam knew it was wrong to eavesdrop. But that wasn't about to stop her!

"Just because Mom and Dad are whispering behind closed doors doesn't necessarily mean they don't want me to hear," she told herself. "Does it?"

She crept down the hall to her parents' bedroom. Then she pressed her ear against the door.

"I think it's wonderful that you want to put Sam on the Hurricanes," Denise was saying.

Me, on the Hurricanes? Sam's heart leaped. It

was what she had wanted ever since Dad started coaching the team!

"But promise me you'll let Emma play, too," Denise added.

"Out of the question!" Jerry said firmly.

"Didn't you hear anything I said last night, Jerry?" Denise said, her voice rising a little. "Emma is dying for a chance to get close to you! If you let Sam play, and not her, she'll be devastated."

"But, Denise..."

"It's not open for discussion!" Denise declared. "Either both girls play, or neither plays! I'm putting my foot down!"

Sam was so busy listening to her parents' conversation that she didn't notice Emma walk up behind her.

"Putting her foot down about what?" Emma asked.

Sam jumped. "Um..." she began.

Just then, Denise opened the bedroom door. "Sam! Emma!" she called at the top of her lungs. Then she looked startled as she saw them. "Oh."

Sam rubbed her ringing ears. "Hi, Mom."

"What's going on?" asked Emma.

Denise grinned. "Your father's soccer league has gone co-ed."

Sam heard her dad groan. Her mom ignored it.

"And he wants to know if you would like to play on his team."

Emma pointed toward Sam. "You mean he wants *her* to play. Right?"

"Yes," said Denise, nodding. "*And* you, Emma. Both of you."

There was another groan from the bedroom. This time, the twins' mother reached behind her and shut the door hard. "Well? What do you think?"

"I think it's totally cool!" said Sam. She turned to Emma, trying not to let her excitement show. She didn't want to make Emma nervous. "What about you, Em? Are you in?"

"Uh…yeah. Sure." A half-hopeful, half-scared expression appeared on Emma's face. "If it's okay with Dad."

"Okay with Dad?" their mom repeated. "Well, of course it's okay with Dad. In fact, it was his idea!" She opened the bedroom door again. "Isn't that right, honey?"

Sam caught a quick glimpse of their dad. He was sprawled on the bed. At the sound of his wife's voice, he quickly sat up and smiled. "You bet!"

Sam knew he wasn't telling the truth. But Emma was beaming, so Sam kept quiet.

Emma on a soccer team, she thought. *How bad could that be?*

She was about to find out.

On Sunday, Emma and Sam made their way toward the playing field. A huge banner announced "EVANSVILLE YOUTH SOCCER LEAGUE TRYOUTS." The twins studied the scene.

"Looks like we're the only girls here," Sam said matter-of-factly.

"Those may be good odds at a school dance," said Emma. She felt a tingle of nervousness. "But I'm not sure I want us to be the only girls in *this* crowd."

Sam laughed. "Lighten up, Em. It'll be fun. Can't you just picture us: Sam and Emma Stanton, stars of the Hurricanes. It's going to be great!"

Emma gave her a doubtful look. "Right."

Both of them turned their attention back to the field. Boys were everywhere, running, passing, and kicking. All of them wore the latest in high-tech soccer gear.

Emma glanced down at her own outfit. She looked like the clearance bin at Jerry's Wide World of Sports. She had on shin guards, like every other kid on the field. But she was also protected by knee pads, shoulder pads, elbow pads, a mouth guard, a bike helmet, and a pair of racquetball goggles.

She caught Sam giving her a funny look. "What?"

"I think you went a little overboard."

Emma checked her gear. "I just wanted to be prepared."

"Emma," Sam sighed. "You're prepared for an earthquake."

Reluctantly, Emma took off everything but the shin guards. "Better?"

"Much!" Sam opened her gym bag so her sister could dump the extra padding into it.

The twins' parents joined them at the edge of the field.

"Nice day for a draft," said their father, scanning the players on the field with narrowed eyes.

"There's no draft, Dad," Emma said, puzzled. "In fact, I was thinking it's kind of warm. I hope I don't start to sweat."

Sam opened her mouth. She looked as if she were about to say something. But then she closed it again. "Come on, Em," she said. She lifted her gym bag onto her shoulder and led her sister across the field. "Let me explain a few things...."

* * *

Denise tapped her husband on the shoulder. Hard. "Excuse me," she said, "but isn't a draft where the good players get chosen first? And the less-talented ones get chosen last?"

"Yeah," Jerry answered. "So?"

"So...you never said anything about a draft."

Jerry gulped. "I didn't?"

"No." His wife folded her arms. "And I don't think I like it. What about the feelings of the kids who are chosen last?"

Jerry frowned. "I don't deal in feelings. I deal in sports. And sports is about finding the best starting lineup you can get."

The twins' mother planted her hands on her hips. "Well, I don't like it."

"Noted." Jerry pointed to the other coaches. They were scattered around the field, making notes on their clipboards. "Now, if you don't mind," he said, "I'm going to check out the athletes." He started to walk away.

"I don't mind at all," Denise said sweetly. "As long as you promise me you'll choose Emma first."

That stopped Jerry in his tracks.

"You *were* planning to pick her first?" his wife called after him. "Weren't you?"

Jerry slowly turned to face her.

Denise frowned. "You weren't going to pick your own daughter first?"

"Of course I was," Jerry said. His gaze slid away. "Just not that daughter," he added in a mumble.

His wife's eyes blazed.

"Come on, Denise," he pleaded. "It's not like Emma's going anywhere. She'll still be available by the third round."

"That's exactly my point!" Denise exclaimed. "The whole purpose of having Emma do this was to bring the two of you closer together. You have to show her that you love her for who she is, not how how well she can play soccer."

"Denise!" Jerry stamped his foot like a little kid. "There's no guarantee Sam will still be around for my next pick!"

"It's a risk you'll have to take. Isn't it?" Denise paused, waiting for an answer.

Her husband threw up his hands. "Girls!" he huffed, and then stomped away.

"Emma just might surprise you!" Denise Stanton called after him.

Just then, she caught sight of Emma. Her daughter had stopped to reapply her lip gloss.

"I hope," Denise muttered.

CHAPTER FOUR

At midfield, Sam got down to business. She skillfully bounced the ball from one knee to the other.

"What are you doing?" asked Emma.

"Warm-up drill," Sam explained. "Want to try?" She used her right knee to punch the ball in her sister's direction.

Determined, Emma picked up the ball. She lifted her left knee and bounced the ball off it.

The ball landed on the ground with a thud. Emma sighed.

"Don't give up," said Sam. She gave her sister's shoulder a squeeze. "Hey, you're new at this. You'll get the hang of it."

Reluctantly, Emma picked up the ball and tried again.

"Not bad," Sam said, with an encouraging smile. "Yeah, that's it. Just concentrate."

For a little while, it looked like Emma was catching on. The ball moved back and forth in a perfectly controlled arc.

"I'm doing it!" she cried. "I've got it!"

But on the next bounce, Emma lifted her knee a little too high. The ball shot off to one side—and nailed another player right in the face.

When Sam saw who her sister had clobbered, she couldn't help grinning. The victim was Richie Jensen, the most competitive kid in the league. He took soccer *very* seriously.

"Oh, no! Did I hurt him?" Emma cried.

"Nah," Sam told her.

Emma fluffed her hair. "Good. Because he's kind of cute."

Richie was heading for them, the ball tucked under his arm. His cheeks were flaming red.

"Sorry about that." Emma tried a little smile.

Richie shoved the ball at Emma.

"Hey," he growled. "Girls don't belong on the soccer field. Why don't you go be a cheerleader or something?"

When he was gone, Sam turned to Emma. "Still think he's cute?"

Emma shrugged. "Well, he'll take some work. He's definitely got crush potential, though."

"Crush?" Sam repeated. "As in, *crush* you into a million pieces, if you ever bop him with the ball again."

She took the ball from Emma and gave it a kick. It sailed into the goal.

After that, practice went from bad to worse for Emma.

Sam was amazing. She wove and dodged through the other players without losing the ball. She slammed free kicks past the goalie. She even stole the ball from Richie a couple of times. After fifteen minutes, all the other players were staring at her in awe. She was one of the best on the field!

Emma, on the other hand, was a disaster. She lost the ball every time she got it. Once she dove for it, but wound up getting tangled in the goal net. It took three coaches to get her out. Richie laughed his head off at that one. Sam offered to slug him, but Emma said no.

Finally, it was time to start the draft. The coaches came together at midfield. The athletes formed a circle around them. Mr. Eldridge, the league coordinator, gave a loud blast on his whistle.

"All right, coaches," he began. "You've seen the players. Time to make your choices." He turned to Sam and Emma's dad. "Last year's winning coach, Jerry Stanton, will have the honor of making the first pick."

From the sidelines, Denise threw her husband a look of warning.

Jerry's eyes darted anxiously from Emma to Sam, then back to Emma. Emma looked so worried. So hopeful. So trusting.

Sam, on the other hand, looked like a kid who could win the Hurricanes another league title.

His coaching instincts were screaming, "Sam!" She was a sure thing.

But Emma would be heartbroken if he overlooked her. He knew Emma needed him. Even more than the Hurricanes needed a star forward.

Jerry drew a deep breath. "The Hurricanes pick...Emma Stanton!"

For a moment, the field was dead silent.

Emma took a step forward. Then she immediately stepped back. "Are you sure, Dad?" she asked. "You want to pick *me*?"

"I'm positive," Jerry said. He glanced over his shoulder at his wife. Then he turned back to smile at Emma. "Believe me, this one's a no-brainer."

As Emma proudly took her place beside her father, Jerry noticed something. The other coaches were staring at Sam. They looked like hungry hyenas, ready to pounce. Obviously, they'd noticed her performance during the practice session.

He thought fast. "Uh, Sam...is that nasty ankle sprain still giving you trouble?" he said loudly.

The other coaches raised their eyebrows.

Sam gave her father a blank look. "What ankle sprain?"

Jerry turned to his colleagues, shaking his head. "She's such a trooper," he said. "She never knows when that injury is going to put her on the bench. And she pretends she doesn't even remember it."

It was the next coach's turn to choose. The coach of the Raiders looked at Sam and her ankle. Then he pointed to a skinny kid with knobby knees. "Frankie Rodriguez," he said. "Welcome to the Raiders."

One by one, the rest of the remaining coaches chose their first new player. Jerry gave a sigh of relief. His bluff about Sam's ankle had scared them off. And now it was his turn again.

He held out his arms to Sam. "Come to Daddy!" he said joyfully.

"Hey, guys, wait up!"

Everyone turned around. A heavyset man in a Hawaiian shirt was jogging toward them. At least, he was trying to jog. His big, blubbery belly seemed to be slowing him down. Jerry recognized the newcomer as Willard Holmes. Willard had been coaching his team, the Buzzards, for years. He hadn't won a game yet.

"Just in time, Willard," Mr. Eldridge said. "Go ahead and pick."

"Whoa, whoa! Wait a minute!" Jerry cried. "What happened to rules? We're on the second round already."

Mr. Eldridge frowned. "Relax, Stanton. Where's your sense of fair play? The guy's only a few minutes late."

"Yeah, but—"

Mr. Eldridge gave a loud blast on his whistle. "Choose, Willard."

Willard looked around at all of the athletes. "Well," he began. He pulled a candy bar from his shirt pocket and tore off the wrapping. "We *are* co-ed this year. My mama always said, 'ladies first,' so..." He took a huge bite of his candy. Then he pointed his chocolate-smudged finger into the crowd of players. "How about that young lady right there?"

Jerry closed his eyes in despair.

Willard's pudgy finger was pointing straight at Sam!

CHAPTER FIVE

Sam sulked all afternoon and all night. She sulked right through breakfast, and then through the entire bus ride to school.

"I'm a Buzzard," she said, over and over. She couldn't believe it. "I wanted to be a Hurricane, but I'm a Buzzard."

"Cheer up," Emma told her. "I had to sit through Dad's lecture on the joy of sweat. He actually made me do a sit-up."

Sam was still sulking when she met Emma for lunch in the cafeteria. As they moved through the line with their trays, though, Sam saw something that made her forget all about soccer for a moment. "Oh, no," she muttered.

"What?" Emma asked, choosing a salad. "Did you forget your milk?"

"No, but I think I'm about to toss my cookies," Sam replied. "There's Greg Jacobs."

Emma turned around. "Greg Jacobs?" She took a fruit cup from the cooler. "What about him?"

Sam grabbed a salad, too. "Uh...nothing."

"Yeah," said Emma. She gave her sister a sideways look. "He's nothing, all right."

Sam frowned. "What do you mean, he's nothing? Some girls think he's totally hot."

"Hot?" Emma hid her grin. "Lukewarm, maybe. I'll even give you toasty, but—"

"Toasty?" snapped Sam. "Try sizzling! Try explosive! Try—"

"Nuclear meltdown?" Emma giggled.

Sam was confused. "So you *do* think he's hot?"

Now Emma was laughing out loud. "Of course I do. Greg Jacobs is why fire alarms were invented!" She gave Sam a friendly elbow to the ribs. "I just wanted to hear *you* say it!"

"He's smart, too," Sam said, paying the lunch lady. "And nice. And"—suddenly, her eyes widened with terror—"he's on his way over here right now!"

Emma handed her money to the lunch lady and rolled her eyes. "Relax, Sam. He's just a guy!"

"Easy for *you* to say." Sam looked down at her tray. "You actually talk to them."

When Greg appeared beside them, Sam hoped he wouldn't notice that her hands were trembling.

"Hi, Emma." Greg didn't even glance at Sam.

Sam wanted to shrink down to the size of a bean

sprout and hide in her salad bowl. She could feel Emma shoot her an apologetic look. That only made her feel worse.

"Hi," Emma said smoothly. She nudged Sam toward Greg. "Hey, you know my sister, don't you?"

Greg looked at Sam. "Right. Hi...uh, Pam, is it?"

"Actually," Sam mumbled, "it's Sam."

"Oh. Yeah." Greg shrugged. "Sorry."

"Aren't you two in the same homeroom?" Emma asked. This time she moved Sam forward with a good hard shove.

"Are we?" said Greg, sounding uninterested.

"Uh-huh," Sam said, nodding. "I sit three rows behind you. Two seats to your left." She swallowed hard. "Uh, not that I ever counted or anything."

Greg smiled politely. Then he turned his attention back to Emma. "Well, I've got to get to English class," he said. Then he gave Emma the cutest wink Sam had ever seen. "Hope I see you around."

"Thanks for introducing me," Sam said when Greg was gone. "But I don't think it worked. He still has no clue who I am."

"Hey, you're new at this," Emma said. "You'll get the hang of it." She gave her twin's shoulder a squeeze. "Sound familiar?"

Sam nodded, remembering Emma on the soccer

27

field. "Like you and the soccer ball," she said. Then she smiled. "You know what would be a lot easier than talking to Greg? Kicking him around in the grass!"

After school, Emma met her dad at the field for the Hurricanes' first practice. He was unloading a big cardboard carton from the back of the van.

"Hey, Emma, look what I've got!" he yelled. He reached into the box. "Jerseys!"

Emma stared in horror at the shirt her father held up.

"Blue and white?" She shook her head. "Forget it, Dad. You're not getting me into one of those. White makes me look pale. And that blue competes with the color of my eyes."

"Emma," said Jerry. He closed his eyes to gather his patience. "These are the Hurricane colors. You've heard our cheer: 'We're the white, We're the blue, Mess with us, Your team is through!'"

"Oh, that's lovely, Dad." Emma wrinkled her nose. "The cheer is as gross as the jerseys!"

Her father shook his head. Then he went back to lugging equipment out of the van.

"Hey!" came a voice from midfield. "You!"

Emma turned around. Richie, the goalie, was

pointing at her. Instinctively, she fluffed her hair.

"Hi, Richie," she said, heading toward him.

But Richie didn't return the greeting. Instead, he scowled at her. "I'm only going to say this once. We Hurricanes take our soccer seriously, so you'd better be ready to work. Don't think you can just stand around looking pretty, just because you're the coach's daughter!"

With that, he turned and stomped away. Emma stared after him in dismay.

Her dad came up beside her. "What was *that* about?" he asked.

Emma sighed. "Your ultracompetitive goalie is having a hard time getting in touch with his romantic side."

Jerry rolled his eyes. "You're starting to sound like your mother."

Then Emma thought of something that made her feel a little better. "But he does think I'm pretty!"

"That's very important for winning."

Emma ignored the sarcasm. She was already digging into the carton. She needed to find a jersey that wasn't totally enormous.

"The oversized look has been out for ages, Dad," she explained. She held up a jersey that hung almost to her knees. Then she dropped it back in the box. "Could you order me a petite?"

"Petite?" Jerry shook his head.

"Yes," said Emma. "And while you're at it, how about changing the whole color scheme? Pink and cream stripes would be perfect. Because I've got this great hot-pink nail polish. And you can lose that nasty old cheer. We could come up with a new one. You know, maybe something like...Let's see....'Here come the Hurricanes in pink and cream, The goalie for the other team sure is a dream!'"

For a moment, her father just stared at her. Then he reached into the carton again. He pulled out a large-sized jersey and handed it to his daughter.

"Wear it in good health, honey," he said. Then he lifted the carton and carried it out to midfield. The rest of the players began pulling out jerseys.

Emma stared at the hideous piece of clothing in her hand. "Calvin Klein needs to come out with a line of soccer uniforms," she said with a sigh.

Sam stood on the sidelines. She was glumly checking out her teammates on the field.

"It's Geeks R Us!" she muttered.

One kid was wearing strange dental headgear. Another guy ran as if he had spiders in his underwear. One of the kids wore a football helmet. And

30

the goalie was smeared from head to toe with thick, white sunblock.

"Casper the Friendly Goalie," Sam grumbled. She frowned as he missed an easy one. "The ball goes right through him."

Miserably, she began to stretch on the grass.

"What are you doing?" said a voice above her.

Sam looked up to see the headgear kid. His metal braces caught the sun. It almost blinded her.

"I'm warming up," she answered, shading her eyes.

Headgear Kid held out his hand. "Well, I'm Oscar," he said. "I wanted to welcome you to the Buzzards."

Sam managed a smile. "Thank you," she said. She shook Oscar's hand.

The sunblock-smeared goalie appeared at Oscar's side. He smelled like coconut oil. "I'm Jeffrey," he said. "Nice to have you on the team."

"Uh...thanks." Sam cleared her throat. "It's nice to be here," she added as sincerely as she could. She was beginning to feel a little guilty for thinking these guys were geeks. They seemed kind of nice.

Jeffrey handed her a jersey. "Here."

"You're one of us now," Oscar declared.

At that, the rest of the players approached from

the field. They began to cheer, "One of us... One of us... One of us..." at the top of their lungs.

Sam didn't know whether to find it touching or terrifying. Looking at the jersey in her hand, she decided on terrifying. The name of the team's sponsor was printed in big block letters across the back: PLAINVIEW FUNERAL HOME.

"How depressing," she muttered. Then, she saw the hurt expression on Jeffrey's face. She quickly pulled the green jersey over her head. "I mean, how...appropriate."

Behind his headgear, Oscar looked confused. "Appropriate?"

"Yeah," said Sam. "Because...um, we're going to *bury* our opponents! Yeah. That's it."

To Sam's relief, the Buzzards applauded.

"Well, we've never actually beaten anyone before," Jeffery said. "But it doesn't hurt to think positive."

"Right. Positive," Sam said. She looked down at the scrawny buzzard logo on her jersey. "I'm *positive* this will be the longest soccer season of my life," she added under her breath.

CHAPTER SIX

After practice, Emma and Sam met at Slappy's to compare notes.

Slappy's was the most popular hangout in town. Sam liked it because the pizza was double cheesy. Emma liked it because they served fat-free salad dressing.

When Emma arrived, she found Sam playing her favorite video game.

"So how did it go?" Sam asked. She didn't take her eyes off the screen.

Emma groaned. "Let me put it this way. If I broke a nail on a bad hair day during which a huge zit suddenly appeared in the middle of my forehead, and I found out I had incurable bad breath, I couldn't feel any worse." She watched as Sam expertly chopped her video enemy's head off. "How about you?"

"Well, let's see," Sam said. "First there's the kid who insists on wearing a football helmet to protect his head. Then we've got a kid who wears enough sunblock to cause a solar eclipse, and a kid with dental equipment that picks up twelve out-of-state radio stations."

Emma wrinkled her nose. "Not exactly your dream team, huh?"

"Not exactly." Sam hit a button and blew up an entire band of evil ninjas to win the game. "So how was Dad?"

Emma shook her head and headed for a booth. Sam followed.

"Well, he tried to act like he was glad to have me there," Emma began. "But I could tell he doesn't really want me." She slid into the seat and frowned. "Every time I made a mistake he made me run a lap." She put her elbows on the tabletop and rested her chin in her hands. "I guess I was kind of hoping that having Dad for a coach would help me learn to be a jock. Then maybe we'd be closer. I really wanted to make him proud of me. But it doesn't look like that's going to happen."

The waitress arrived. Emma ordered a small salad and a mineral water.

"Nothing for me, thanks," said Sam.

"*Nothing*?" Emma stared at her twin. "Who are you, and what have you done with my sister?"

Sam rolled her eyes. "Coach Willard likes to discuss game strategy over pizza. He has it delivered right to the field." She leaned back in her seat. "Not what I'd call a world-class coaching technique. It was sort of sweet the way he helped Oscar pick the anchovies out of his headgear, though."

"Did you even get to play?"

Sam shook her head. "Nope. We just sat around and did nothing. I ate so much pizza I feel sick."

Emma's calves were beginning to hurt. "Maybe you'd be better off playing for Dad."

"Well, you'd definitely be better off playing for Willard." Sam grinned at the salad the waitress had placed in front of Emma. "I bet he'd even order you a salad."

"Sounds nice," Emma murmured. "If only—"

She sat up straight as an idea hit her. Her eyes locked with Sam's, and she could tell her twin was thinking the same thing. It was as if the same idea had popped into both their minds at once.

"You don't think we could..." Sam started.

"We might be able to pull off a..." Emma began.

"Switch!" they finished together.

For a second Emma felt hopeful. Then she thought of something. She speared a radish with her fork.

"I don't know. This might be my only chance to

bond with Dad." She sighed. "Then again, if I keep playing as badly as I did today, he might disown me."

"I bet we *could* pull off a switch," Sam said. "If we wanted to."

Emma crunched the radish, then twirled a piece of lettuce. "Oh, definitely. It would be easy. Remember that time in second grade?"

"Sure." Sam laughed. "I didn't want to go to Candace Collins's Barbie Bash Sleepover. You didn't want to trek through the wilderness with your Brownie troop. So we switched places. It worked out great."

"Switching, huh?" Emma munched a mushroom as she thought some more about the idea. It sure would make life easier.

"I bet Dad wouldn't mind having me on the team," said Sam. "Sorry. Nothing personal."

"I know." Emma smiled. "He'd trade you, too, if he thought it gave him a better shot at winning."

"Right. And Willard—he'd probably never notice."

Emma frowned. "You know who *would* notice, though?"

"Mom," they both said at the same time.

Sam nodded. "She'll come to all the games," she

said. "Buzzards and Hurricanes. We'd never be able to sneak it past her."

Emma picked up a carrot stick and snapped it in half. "Bummer."

"Oh, well," Sam said glumly. "I guess I'm still a Buzzard."

"And I'm stuck in the middle of a Hurricane."

Sam scowled. "Unless we just..."

"...quit," Emma finished for her. It was beginning to seem like their only choice.

Sam slapped her palm against the tabletop. "No fair! I was really looking forward to playing in a co-ed league." She waved the waitress over. "I'd like an order of nachos," she said. "And a large onion rings, a strawberry shake..."

"I thought you said you weren't hungry," Emma reminded her.

"I have to drown my sorrows in something," Sam said. "It might as well be food." She turned back to the waitress. "And a brownie-bomb sundae with extra whipped cream for dessert."

Emma hesitated a moment. "Make that two," she said.

Sam leaned forward. "You do realize that a brownie-bomb sundae is not a low-fat item?"

Emma reached down to rub her aching legs. "I

must have run eight zillion miles today," she said in a pained voice. "I think I'm due for a few calories."

When the sundaes arrived, the girls devoured them in gloomy silence.

Even the extra whipped cream didn't help.

"Mom's never been big on quitting," Emma said softly.

"We don't have a choice," Sam whispered back.

The girls were standing outside the door to their mother's home office. It was time to tell her they were quitting co-ed soccer.

Sam took a deep breath and opened the door. Denise was seated at her desk, doing paperwork.

"Hi, Mom. Got a minute?" Sam asked.

Denise smiled. "For you two? Always!" She stood up and came around to the front of her desk. "Actually, there's something I need to tell you. I have some disappointing news. As much as I was looking forward to seeing you two play...well, I'm not going to be able to come to any of your games."

"*Any* of them?" Sam repeated. Hope bubbled up inside her.

"I got a call this morning from Dr. Wesley at the clinic. My Family Dynamics seminar has been moved to Saturday mornings. And since you play on Saturdays..."

The girls exchanged glances. Sam could tell her twin was thinking the same thing. With Mom working every Saturday, they were free to switch teams!

"I'm so sorry," Denise said. "Do you mind very much?"

"Not at all," Emma told her mother.

"It's okay," Sam said. She fought back the urge to cheer. "We know you can't help it."

Denise smiled warmly. "I knew you'd understand."

"We do," said Sam. "We totally understand."

"Yeah," said Emma. "We know how important that Family Dynamite stuff is to you."

Mom laughed. "It's Family Dynamics. Speaking of which, how did practice go? Was Dad supportive? Did he use positive mentoring skills?"

"Oh, sure. There's never been a more positive mentor than Dad," Emma fibbed. Sam could see her twin flexing one cramping calf muscle.

"I'm so glad to hear that." Denise turned to Sam. "And how was Coach Willard?"

Sam cleared her throat. "Well," she said, "If you've got a real appetite for sports, Willard's your man."

"Excellent." Their mother nodded her approval.

"Now, what was it you wanted to tell me?"

Again, the girls exchanged looks.

"Um…" said Emma.

"Uh…" Sam stalled.

"We were just wondering…"

Sam jumped in with a bluff. "…if you know how many laps of the soccer field it takes to burn off a brownie-bomb sundae with extra whipped cream."

Denise gave them a blank look. "Excuse me?"

"It's a riddle," said Sam quickly. "You know. Like how many psychologists does it take to change a lightbulb?"

"Oh." Denise thought for a moment. "I give up. How many laps *does* it take to burn off those calories?"

There was a moment of awkward silence. Suddenly, Emma grinned and announced, "None!"

"None?"

"Correct!" cried Sam. She gave Emma a wink. "Because when you're on the right team, you don't need ice cream!"

Emma and Sam both broke into a fit of giggles. Denise didn't get the joke at all.

CHAPTER SEVEN

"What do you mean, 'switch?'" Jerry asked. He and the twins were talking that afternoon at the Wide World of Sports.

"We mean," Sam said, "I'll play for you as Emma. And Emma can play for Willard. As me."

Jerry raised his eyebrows. "Switch, huh?" He hesitated, looking tempted. Then he shook his head. "No. No way, girls. It's too risky." He turned to Emma. "I'm sorry if I was rough on you yesterday. I promise, I'll back off."

"That's sweet of you to say, Dad," Emma said. She plucked a tennis skirt from a nearby rack and held it up against her. "But let's face it. Me? A Hurricane? I don't think so."

"And I can't take being a Buzzard," Sam put in. "Those guys wouldn't know a soccer ball if they tripped over one. And they usually do!"

"I see the point." Jerry tapped one finger against his chin. "But switching...it doesn't sound very sportsmanlike."

Emma thought fast. "Don't think of it as a switch," she advised. "It's a"—she turned to Sam— "what's it called, in the major leagues?"

"A trade," Sam said.

Jerry scratched his chin. "You want to trade yourselves?"

"Isn't it brilliant?" Emma checked out the top that matched the skirt. If she got traded to the Buzzards, she could easily skip some practices and fit in a few tennis dates. Not that she played very well. But in this cute outfit, who'd notice? She smiled at her dad. "Everyone gets what they want."

"A trade," said Jerry slowly. "Now that sounds more like it." He frowned. "But what about your mom? It's not the kind of thing she'd go for."

"Who says Mom has to find out?" said Sam in a casual voice.

When their dad's frown deepened, Emma hurried to explain. "We were going to tell her things weren't working out. But then *she* told *us* she has to work every Saturday. She can't come to any games. She'll never know which twin is on which team. In fact, nobody has to know. It can be our secret."

Jerry paced back and forth between the racks. "Sounds like you've got it all figured out."

"We do," said Sam. "We've even got practice

alibis. On days when the Buzzards practice, Emma will go as me, and I'll hide out in the library. On Hurricane practice days, I'll go as me, and Emma goes to the library."

Emma glanced at her father. He didn't seem sold. She decided to bring out the big guns.

She waved her hand toward the wall where the Hurricanes' awards were displayed. "Dad, this is bigger than all of us. Think of the Hurricanes. Think of your reputation."

Jerry stopped pacing. "I hope you're not doing this for my sake. I know you think I'm obsessed with winning. But I'm not. I mean, it may seem that way sometimes, but…"

The girls shot each other a look.

"*You*?" Sam said. "Obsessed with winning?"

"No way, Dad." Emma said. "We know you play for fun."

"I do?" Jerry caught himself. "I mean, yes, of course I do. And if you two aren't having fun…well, then, a trade makes perfect sense."

Sam broke into a huge grin. Emma had to hide her face in a pair of boxing gloves to keep from laughing out loud.

The deal was done!

* * *

The next few days of practice went even better than the girls had hoped.

Sam, pretending to be Emma, played her heart out at the Hurricanes' workout sessions. Even Richie couldn't ignore "Emma's" sudden skill. On the day before the first game, he confronted her.

"What happened to you?" he demanded. Sam had just sent a fourth ball screaming by him into the goal.

"Gee, I don't know," said Sam. She kept a straight face. "Maybe it's my new breakfast cereal. Or maybe..." She tried to think of what the real Emma might say. "Maybe watching a big, strong, talented athlete like you has inspired me."

Richie opened his mouth to reply, then snapped it shut. Sam noticed his cheeks turn pink.

After that, Richie couldn't stop a single ball for the rest of practice.

Hmm, Sam thought. *Maybe flirting isn't totally useless, after all.*

The next day, Emma had just as much fun at the Buzzards' practice.

She helped Willard with the team's warm-up by leading the Electric Slide at midfield. Then she joined in Willard's famous Conga Line Dribble Drill.

After that, the rest of the team made dopes of themselves trying to scrimmage. Emma sat on the sidelines, working on her tan.

She settled back in the beach chair Jeffrey had brought for her. Then she reached into the team cooler for her low-calorie fruit-flavored iced tea. From her gym bag, she removed a small makeup case. She needed to check her hair in her mirror.

"It isn't whether you win or lose," Emma told herself. She took a sip of iced tea. "It's how great you look at the game!"

On Saturday, the Hurricanes had their first game against the Bulls. The team was playing well, but they weren't winning. With thirty seconds left, each team had scored twice.

Jerry called a time-out. His players huddled on the sideline. "The score is tied!" he barked. "A tie is not a win!"

Dave, who was the assistant coach, nodded in agreement. So did all of the Hurricanes.

"So, here's the plan," Jerry said. "We run Play 32." He turned to his daughter. "Sam—I mean, Emma—you flank the striker. Break out of the pack when Andy centers the ball by the goal. Ready? Break!"

The players jogged back onto the field. But Richie caught "Emma" by the arm.

"Talk about playing favorites!" he said with a scowl. "Your dad's running a play for you so you won't cry all weekend. He's risking the whole game just to keep your mascara from running."

Sam planted her hands on her hips and glared at Richie. "First of all, my mascara doesn't run. *I* do. Faster than you, I might add. And second, what makes you think I can't handle this play? You saw me at practice yesterday." She gave him a sarcastic smile. "Or maybe you didn't. I was probably just a blur."

The screech of Jerry's whistle ended the argument. Sam and Richie ran to their places.

"'Mascara my foot," Sam muttered. Another whistle blew, and she expertly moved into position. She was so furious at Richie that she hardly even noticed the herd of Bulls heading for her. She stayed focused, weaving through their defense, hunting for a clear spot on the field.

With seven seconds left on the clock, Andy centered the ball and prepared to pass to "Emma."

The ball headed toward Sam in a smooth arc. But it was high. It looked as if it would go right over her head.

From the sidelines, Jerry and Dave groaned. "Too high! Too high!"

But Sam wasn't going to let that bother her. She threw herself skyward and swung one leg up. WHAM! Her foot connected with the ball. The thump echoed across the field.

She landed gracefully in the grass. The ball continued to fly at top speed—straight into the goal net. A second later, the buzzer sounded.

A huge roar rose from the Hurricanes' bench. Dave almost sobbed with joy. He jumped into Jerry's arms.

Andy hurried over to Sam. He held out his hand to help her up. "Nice going, Emma. I never thought you had it in you."

"Yeah," said Sam. She brushed the dirt from her shorts. "You're not the only one." She glanced back at the goal at the other end of the field. A reluctant grin flashed across Richie's face.

Her teammates ran to congratulate her.

"Way to go, Emma!"

"Emma, that was awesome!"

Sam beamed and accepted their high-fives. *This is great!* she thought. And then, a moment later: *I wonder how the real Emma is doing?*

* * *

Emma was doing much better than expected!

But only by accident.

The Buzzards were losing to the Corporate Raiders, 15-0. No surprise there. Emma, pretending to be Sam, had been in almost the entire game. Happily, she stayed as far out of play as she could. She passed the time checking out the cutest Raiders.

Then it happened.

Emma was standing near the Raiders' goal. Before she knew it, her teammate Ward passed the ball to her. Actually, he tripped over his shoelace and slipped, but by sheer luck, his foot connected with the ball.

The ball flew in Emma's direction. It landed right at her feet. It was just begging to be kicked.

At first, Emma just stared at it. She had been completely distracted by the Raider goalie's sparkling green eyes. It took her a moment to remember why she was there.

"You might as well kick it!" Willard called from the sidelines. "It can't hurt."

But just as Emma drew her foot back to kick, the goalie burst out of the goal. He bared his teeth, screaming like a madman. He was heading straight for her!

Emma screamed, too. But it was a scream of terror. There was only one way to defend herself: Kick him in the shins.

She drew back her foot and kicked. But before it hit his shin, her foot hit the ball—and hard! To Emma's shock, the ball slammed into the goalie's gut.

"Umfff!" His jaw dropped. Then his green eyes opened wide, and he doubled over.

The ball fell away from his stomach.

It rolled...and rolled...

...slowly...slowly...

...right into the goal!

Emma blinked in shock.

Loud cheering arose from the Buzzards' bench.

"She did it!" Oscar cried. "Sam broke our three year scoreless streak!"

Emma looked at the scoreboard at the far end of the field. The number "1" had appeared beneath the Buzzards' name for the first time ever.

Willard shook up a can of root beer. He popped the top, and sprayed soda foam into the sky. "Whoo-hoo!" he yelled.

Emma's teammates began to chant, "Sam scored! Sam scored! Sam scored!" They met her at midfield and hoisted her onto their shoulders. They could hold her for only two seconds before they collapsed under the strain. But Emma didn't mind. She was too busy enjoying the moment.

Then she thought of something even more exciting. Maybe—just maybe—the green-eyed goalie would get his wind back in time to ask for her phone number.

In the next few weeks, Sam led the Hurricanes to four more victories. Emma managed not to injure any more of her opponents. Four games later, the Hurricanes had a record of four wins and no losses. The Buzzards' record stood at no wins and four losses.

At games, Jerry heard the other coaches discussing his team's success. They asked him how he'd turned "Emma" into an instant all-star. He told them that it had everything to do with the right equipment. And all of it could be bought for a low, low price at Jerry's Wide World of Sports.

After that, a very tired Dave sold more soccer equipment in one week than he had in his entire sports-store career.

It seemed as if everyone had what they wanted.

But the season wasn't over yet!

CHAPTER EIGHT

On Monday afternoon, Sam picked up her gym bag and headed out the front door to soccer practice. Normally, since Monday was a Hurricanes practice day, Emma and Sam would have walked out together and then switched bags once they were clear of the house. But today the coast was clear, since the girls' mom was at the market.

At least, she was *supposed* to be at the market. So what was she doing coming up the walk toward Sam?

"Sam, where are you going?"

"Uh..." The gym bag suddenly seemed to weigh a thousand pounds. "To the library. I—I thought you were shopping."

"My last appointment cancelled, so I went shopping early." Denise put the grocery bag down on the porch. Then she peeked into Sam's open duffel. "Since when do you need soccer shoes to study?" she asked.

Sam gulped. "Soccer shoes?" She forced a laugh.

"Well, what do you know? That *is* my soccer stuff. I thought I grabbed my backpack. You know, with my pencils and schoolbooks..."

Her mother gave her a doubtful look.

Then Emma bounded out to the porch. She was carrying a backpack. "Hey, goofball!" she said to Sam. "You grabbed the wrong bag!"

It took Sam a minute, but then she caught on.

Emma shoved her own backpack into Sam's hand. Then she pulled Sam's gym bag onto her shoulder. "There, that's better," she chirped. "Now you can go to the library, and I can go practice with the Hurricanes. Bye, Mom."

They were halfway down the walk when their mom stopped them with an "Excuse me...."

The girls stopped in their tracks.

"Emma, why are you taking Sam's gym bag to practice?"

"Um..." Emma stalled. She cleared her throat.

"Because," Sam said quickly, "I am such a sweet, kind, generous twin sister, I've agreed to let Emma wear my stuff during practice."

Denise frowned. "Why?"

Sam thought fast. "For luck. We thought maybe some of my athletic ability would rub off on her if she wore my uniform."

"Yeah," Emma said. "Don't worry, Mom. All Sam's stuff fits me because we're twins."

"Yes," Denise said. "I remember. I was there when you were born."

"Right. Well, anyway..." Sam sputtered. "See you!" The girls turned and continued quickly down the walk.

"Not so fast," their mom called. "Sam, isn't that Emma's backpack?"

Busted!

"Yes, as a matter of fact, it is."

"How are you going to do your homework if you've got Emma's backpack?"

Again, Sam came up with a great excuse. "I never said I was going to the library to do my homework," she said. "I already did *my* homework. Emma did hers, too. The reason I'm bringing Emma's backpack is because—again—I am so sweet, kind, and generous. I've offered to check Emma's homework for her."

"That's right," said Emma. "Gotta go!"

"See you, Mom," Sam called.

Before Denise could say anything else, the girls ran for it.

After practice, Sam sat on the sidelines. She

took off her shin guards and watched her team-mates leaving the field. It had been another great Hurricane practice. Every muscle in her body was tingling. She wore the grass stains on her knees and elbows like badges of honor.

If their mom had figured out their switch, Sam would be back to playing Buzzard ball for sure. That would be the worst drag she could imagine.

A voice from behind her broke into her thoughts. "Emma."

She didn't answer. Whoever it was wasn't talking to her.

"Emma," came the voice again.

She felt a tap on her shoulder. "Emma."

Emma. Right. That's me! Sam whirled around.

Greg Jacobs was standing there. Greg "Nuclear-Meltdown-Who-Doesn't-Know-I'm-Alive" Jacobs.

He smiled. Sam reminded herself not to pass out. Or puke. Or throw her arms around him.

"Greg. Hi."

"So were you just completely ignoring me? Or are you wearing an invisible Walkman?"

Sam managed a chuckle. "Sorry. I guess I didn't hear you."

There was an awkward silence. Now Sam wished she wasn't so covered in grass stains. For all she knew, she had a big clump of dirt on her face, too. "How did you know I was here?" she asked finally.

"I heard you were playing for your dad's team," Greg said. "I thought I'd have a better chance of talking to you if I caught you here after practice. At school you're pretty much always surrounded by other guys."

"Surrounded?" Sam echoed. She gave a jerky giggle. "Oh, yeah. I hate it when that happens."

Greg shoved his hands deep into his pockets nervously. Sam felt better knowing he felt as flustered as she did.

"Uh, are you doing anything Friday night?" he asked.

Sam just shook her head. She couldn't seem to get her voice to work.

"Great. Would you like to go out?"

Sam gulped. "You mean, like on a date?"

Greg nodded.

"With *me*?"

"No," he teased, smiling. "With your twin sister."

For a split second, Sam was going to blurt out the truth. But then she caught herself.

Why not go on with the act? If Greg thought she was Emma, why not let him? She'd pretend to be

Emma for the rest of her life if it meant getting a date with Greg!

"I'd love that," she said. "I mean, I have to ask my parents, but—that would be great."

"Terrific. We could meet at Slappy's at seven, okay?"

"Perfect."

As Greg left, Sam felt a thrill shoot through her. It was sort of like a muscle cramp, only it didn't hurt. She was totally in shock.

She jumped up from the bench. "I have a date with Greg Jacobs!" she said aloud, giggling.

Then she saw Richie, standing a few feet away, glaring at her. He'd probably heard everything she and Greg had said. But Sam was too happy to care. She even smiled at Richie.

For some reason, that made him look even angrier. *What's he so mad about?* she wondered.

But she didn't waste much time wondering about it. All she wanted to think about was Friday night.

And her date with Greg Jacobs.

CHAPTER NINE

At home, Sam ducked quickly into the laundry room and changed out of her grass-stained practice clothes. She couldn't wait to find Emma. She was ready to explode with the news about Greg. And she also had a zillion questions about dating.

She burst into the bedroom. But instead of her sister, she found their mother. She was standing at Emma's dresser, frowning. Sam stopped cold.

Denise was staring at the neatly folded Buzzards jersey in Emma's drawer. Sam thought about bolting. She couldn't, though. Emma, who had just appeared in the doorway, was blocking the exit. Sam could tell that her twin saw the problem at once. They both held their breath.

Without a word, Denise crossed the room. She carefully stepped over Sam's hockey skates and a pillow with the Chicago Bulls logo. She went straight to Sam's dresser and opened a drawer. Then she pulled out a crumpled Hurricanes jersey.

She turned to the twins. There were frown lines

between her eyes. "I never would have believed this."

Oh, no! Sam squeezed her eyes shut.

But their mother actually laughed!

"After twelve years of sorting laundry, I finally slipped up!" She shook her head and folded the Hurricanes jersey. She placed it on Emma's bed. Then she bunched up the Buzzards shirt and dropped it on top of Sam's bureau. "I could have sworn I put them in the right drawers." Suddenly, she looked worried. "Maybe my work is taking up too much of my concentration. Maybe I should cancel my Family Dynamics seminar."

"No!" cried Emma.

"Don't!" said Sam.

"Come on, Mom. It's only a couple of shirts," Emma said.

"Yeah," Sam added. "One mix-up in twelve years. That's a darned good record. You're being way too hard on yourself."

Denise smiled. "I guess you're right. It's just that my special laundry system has always worked."

She stepped back over the pillow, the ball and the skates. With one final, despairing glance at Sam's side of the room, she left.

When she was gone, Emma gave a sigh of relief. "That was close." She headed for her desk.

"What are you doing?"

"Homework."

"Didn't you just spend two hours in the library?"

"Yeah. But half my history class was there. It wound up being a major social thing. I didn't get any work done."

"Well, you won't get any done here, either," Sam told her. She grinned. "Because Greg Jacobs just asked me out for this Friday. So you've got to give me the Emma Stanton Crash Course in making a guy fall madly in love with you on your first date. Tonight, *I'm* your homework!"

After dinner, the girls excused themselves to go upstairs. When they were gone, Denise began to leaf through the newspaper. Suddenly she screamed.

"What?" Jerry Stanton asked.

His wife handed him the sports page. She pointed at an article about the youth soccer league. "Hurricanes Lead League," said the headline.

He'd already read it, of course. A hundred times. But seeing his team's great record in print still brought a smile to his face.

"You didn't tell me the Hurricanes were in first place," his wife said.

Jerry's smile vanished instantly. "I didn't?" He

put the paper down and pretended to be very interested in his dessert. "Hmm. Must have slipped my mind."

Denise folded her arms. "That's not like you. Usually you start bragging before the first victory."

Jerry took a spoonful of pudding. He swallowed hard. "Well, I guess...I guess I'm starting to get a handle on my overcompetitive problem." He gave his wife a grin. "Thanks to you, of course."

For a moment, Denise just stared at him.

"I know what's going on here," she said at last.

Jerry felt the panic rising. "You do?"

"It's obvious." His wife surprised him with a warm smile. "Your coaching skill has made Emma a good player. Your talent has brought out the athlete in her!"

"It has? I mean, yeah...I suppose it has."

"You're a terrific coach, Jerry Stanton. And you're a great father. I knew you'd realize that your relationship with Emma was far more important than winning a few silly soccer games."

"You knew that, huh?" Jerry felt a stab of guilt in his stomach. It didn't mix well with the pudding.

"All along," Denise said. She took away his empty bowl. Then she brought him another pudding. This one had whipped cream and a cherry on top. "And here's a special dessert to show you how proud of you I am."

"Proud. Right."

His wife kissed him on the cheek. Then she went to the sink to start the dishes.

That pudding was the hardest thing he ever had to eat in his life.

Upstairs, Sam was having a hard time, too.

"What do you mean, I can't play video games at Slappy's on Friday night?"

"It's just not a date thing," Emma said.

"Dumb rule." Sam thought for a moment. "What if *he* wants to play a video game?" she asked.

Emma shrugged. "Then I guess that's okay. As long as you let him win at least one game." Before Sam could protest, her twin said, "Let's move on to your walk. Go ahead, let's see it."

Sam walked to the other side of the room. Emma gasped in horror.

"What?" Sam asked. "I made it across, didn't I?"

"Well, sure. You got there, but you didn't look very graceful doing it. Here, watch."

Emma demonstrated. She didn't really walk. She glided. Sam was sure her sister's feet never even touched the floor.

"Now *you* try."

Sam took another crack at it. Glide and sway, glide and sway, glide and...crash! She swayed right into the night-table lamp.

"Oops," she said. She picked up the lamp.

"Don't worry, you'll get it," Emma said. "You're just not used to the shoes."

"Or the dress," Sam added. "Or the earrings, or the hair clips...."

Earlier, Sam went though the quickest fashion makeover in history. She tried on every dress in Emma's closet. After some heated debate, they finally agreed on a simple, light blue tank dress. Emma insisted on plain silver hoop earrings and a delicate ankle bracelet. The eye shadow issue was still under discussion.

But the shoes were the worst. Emma said they were called slip-ons. Sam decided that "slip-offs" was more accurate. She couldn't seem to keep them on her feet.

Sam groaned. "What a waste of time! I'm never going to be able to pull this off. How do you make everything look so easy?"

Emma shrugged. "The same way you make a reverse gainer off the high dive look easy."

"Compared to this, it *is* easy!"

"Let's work on the hair flip," Emma suggested. "Hair flipping strategy is very important. It fills the gap when you're not sure what to say next."

Sam began to panic. "You think I'm going to flub the conversation? You mean I won't know what to talk about?"

"I'm not saying that at all," Emma assured her. "Now, pay attention. The hair flip is a very advanced maneuver."

Emma sat primly on the edge of the bed. She tilted her chin and—*swoosh*—swung her head gracefully to the left. The move sent her shining hair sweeping backwards over her shoulder.

"Wow," said Sam. "When do I do that?"

"Whenever things get too quiet. It dazzles the guy. And it gives you time to think of something cute to say."

Sam made a mental note of that. Then she gave the hair flip a try.

"Not bad," said Emma. She smiled. "I think you're going to do fine on Friday."

Secretly, Sam was not convinced. But she didn't say so. She'd simply have to do the same thing she did when she was trying to perfect a tough new soccer skill. Practice, practice, practice!

CHAPTER TEN

On Friday night, Sam walked into Slappy's at ten minutes past seven. She'd wanted to arrive on time, at seven sharp. But Emma told her that would make her look too eager.

Sam's heart was racing as if she'd just run the hundred-yard dash in record time. But she was able to glide and sway across the restaurant without any problems. Greg was waiting in booth three.

He stood up. "Hi."

"Hi."

"You look great," he said.

"Thank you. Sorry I'm late."

"No problem. I played a few games of Chop off the Old Block."

Sam's eyes lit up. "Really? I love that—"she caught herself. No video game talk! She made a quick save—"shirt. I love that shirt you're wearing. Yeah. Great shirt."

"Thanks."

"You're welcome."

"So how's soccer?"

"Oh, well, you know…" Sam swallowed hard. She would have loved to begin a whole discussion of the sport. But Emma had said no to that. Instead, Sam rolled her eyes and said, "Soccer takes a lot of time away from my shopping."

When the waitress arrived, Sam ordered a salad. Emma had been very clear on that. The cheese on pizza had a sneaky way of sticking to the chin. And salad as a main course just screamed "feminine."

Greg smiled at her. "I'm glad you're here, Emma."

Well, he's half right, Sam thought. She forced a smile. *I'm here.*

I'm just not Emma.

When the food came, Sam ate her salad as carefully as she could. She tried hard to ignore the delicious smell of Greg's pepperoni and pineapple pizza.

"Sure you don't want some?" he asked.

"No, thank you," sighed Sam.

She decided it was time to attempt a hair flip. Unfortunately, she tried it with a piece of carrot in her mouth. She almost choked to death. Greg came through with a thump on her back. But after that, there were several long moments of silence.

"I don't suppose you'd want to play some video games?" Greg said. He sounded a bit desperate.

Sam was out of the booth and halfway to the game before he even finished the question.

"This is the joystick," Greg explained. He slipped a coin into the slot. "Hold it like this." He guided Sam's hand toward the handle. Then he gently wrapped his fingers around hers. "This moves the good guy warrior. Left and right. Like this, see?"

Sam nodded. She knew what the handle was for. She knew every inch of Chop Off the Old Block. But she wasn't going to tell Greg that. This was the closest she'd ever come to holding a boy's hand. It felt wonderful.

"The object of the game is to rescue the emperor from the evil ninjas," Greg went on. "It's hard at first, but..."

He stopped short. Sam's warrior had taken out four ninjas with one kick.

"Whoa," he said.

But Sam barely heard him. Her eyes were on the screen. And her mind was on winning.

Six games later, Greg looked a little dazed.

"You beat me," he said. He sounded shocked.

Sam remembered Emma's advice too late. *Let him win at least one game.* She stepped away from the game as if it were red-hot.

"Nobody's ever beaten me before. Not even once."

"Is that a bad thing?" Sam asked in a tiny voice.

Greg hesitated. "I'm not sure," he said.

Sam bit her lower lip. "Hey, how about dessert? My treat."

Greg shook his head. "No, thanks."

"Are you sure? The brownie-bomb sundae is outrageous."

He cocked an eyebrow at her. "I thought you only ate salad."

"Yeah, well, I...uh..." She trailed off, defeated. *I just blew it all the way, didn't I?* she thought. *Now he thinks I'm a pig on top of everything else.*

Greg stared at her. Sam wished she could tell what he was thinking.

"Ready to go?" he said at last.

Crushed, Sam nodded.

"Man, Emma," Greg said. He held the restaurant door open for her. "You sure are different than I thought you would be."

That definitely sounds like a bad thing, Sam thought glumly.

They walked all the way home without a word.

CHAPTER ELEVEN

On Monday, Sam went to practice with the Hurricanes as usual, and Emma headed to the library.

Unfortunately, on this Monday, Denise went to the library, too.

"Emma?"

Emma looked up from where she'd been doodling in her notebook. Her throat constricted. "Mom! What are you doing here?"

"I'm doing some research for my seminar." Denise checked her watch. "But there's a more important question. What are *you* doing here? Don't the Hurricanes have practice?"

Emma snapped her fingers. "I knew I forgot something. Thanks for reminding me." She stuffed her books into her backpack. "I'll run there now."

"Don't be silly. I'll drive you," Denise said.

As her mom headed out of the library, Emma sent up a silent prayer: Please let Dad be wearing his shin guards! And maybe a mouth guard. And some shoulder pads. And a football helmet, too.

Come to think of it, she and Sam could probably do with some padding of their own.

Denise pulled the car up to the field. Emma hopped out almost before it stopped.

"Bye, Mom. Thanks for the ride."

But to Emma's horror, her mother got out of the car, too. "I'm coming with you," she said.

Emma's heart dropped. "Why?"

"Well, I haven't even seen one game. The least I can do is watch you practice."

"That's okay, Mom," said Emma quickly. "Dad gets cranky when outsiders show up at practice."

Mom laughed. "Em, I'm not an outsider. I'm his wife." She headed toward the field.

In the distance, a golden-haired player was about to nail a goal.

Denise squinted toward the field. "Emma, am I crazy? Or does that kid look an awful lot like you?"

Emma groaned. Defeated, she followed her mom the rest of the way to the sidelines. Jerry had his back to them. He was cheering on his star.

"Way to go! Show no mercy! No mercy! No—"

Emma watched helplessly as her dad received a firm tap on his shoulder. He turned slowly. Then he finished his chant in a pitiful squeak: ". . . mercy?"

Denise glared at him. "Funny you should mention mercy," she said through clenched teeth. "Because you won't get any from me."

Emma's eyes met Sam's across the field. Sadly, Sam shook her head. She finished her play by quickly slamming the ball into the goal.

Emma didn't blame her twin. It might be the last chance Sam got.

At home that evening, Sam and Emma exchanged jerseys. Sam stared down at the Buzzard shirt. "I can't believe this is happening!"

"Well, it was fun while it lasted," Emma said. She wrinkled her nose at the grass stains on Sam's former shirt.

"Why couldn't it have lasted longer?" Sam moaned. "I mean, just yesterday, I was on a super team. I also had a shot at getting a great guy to fall for me. Now it's all over." She gave a huge sigh.

"How do you think *I* feel?" Emma asked. "I'm the one who has to deal with that Richie kid. When he finds out I'm really me and not you, he's going to hate me even more than he did when he thought you were me. Because now I'm really not you, and he hated me even before he believed you were me."

Sam flopped down on her bed and threw the Buzzards jersey over her face. "You know what's really scary?" she asked.

"What?"

"I actually understood that."

"At least we don't have it as bad as Dad," Emma said. "He's got to confess to Mr. Eldridge and the other coaches about what we did."

"That is pretty bad," Sam agreed. There was a long pause.

"I guess there's only one thing for us to do," said Emma. "Quit."

"Unfortunately," Sam said, "I think you're right."

There was a knock at the door. Jerry stuck his head in.

"Hey, girls."

"Are you out of the league?" Emma asked.

"Believe it or not, no. I can keep coaching."

"Really?" Sam pulled the jersey off her face. "Just like that?"

"Well, there is a slight penalty." Jerry said. "The Hurricanes have to forfeit their first four wins."

Sam sat up and blinked. "You call that a *slight* penalty?"

"I don't," said Jerry. "They do."

Sam knew their father would rather give up an

arm than a win. She felt really, really sorry for him.

"What about us?" Emma asked.

Jerry shrugged. "You two can go back to your original teams."

Sam flopped backwards again. "We can," she said. "But we're not going to."

The twins' father looked from one girl to the other. "What do you mean?"

"We're quitting," Emma said. "That's what we should have done in the first place."

"I'm no Buzzard," said Sam.

"And it's not fair to the Hurricanes to have me making so many mistakes," Emma said.

"Emma's right, Dad. If we had just quit right from the start, you wouldn't have had to go through the embarrassment of telling the other coaches. And Mom wouldn't be giving you the silent treatment."

Their dad smiled. "It's not as bad you think, girls. The other coaches were good sports about it."

He tousled Sam's hair. Then he put an arm around Emma's shoulder. "We'll make this work," he said. "You'll be a Hurricane yet, kiddo. Trust me."

"And I'll be a Buzzard," muttered Sam. "Great."

CHAPTER TWELVE

Jerry Stanton was true to his word.

The first thing he did at practice the next day was turn over the coaching responsibilities to Dave. He wanted to work one-on-one with Emma.

They decided that her biggest problem was her kicking. Every time she tried, she missed. The only thing she kicked was huge clumps of dirt. All over the field, little mounds of grass were dying.

"I'm not only bad for the team," Emma said sadly. "I'm bad for the environment."

"Never say die," her dad told her. They kept at it.

The two of them worked on defensive skills without much success. Emma wasn't much better at offense, either.

Jerry decided to call it a day. Emma leaned down to press the grass back into its holes. Then she saw Greg approaching from the sidelines.

"Wonderful," she muttered. "This is all I need."

From what Sam told her, the date had been a disaster. But when she took a closer look at Greg,

Emma began to wonder. He looked interested.

For Sam's sake, she decided to play it cool.

"Hi, Emma," said Greg. He frowned at the holes scattered across the grass. "What happened?"

"Gophers," Emma said flatly. She watched as Greg nervously stuffed his hands in his pockets.

"Listen," he said, "are you busy Saturday?"

"I have a game," Emma said.

"Oh. Well, how about if we get together after it?"

Emma pretended to think it over. Before she could give him another no, Greg spoke.

"I don't know about you, Emma. But I had an excellent time on our date. I admit, I was a little shocked when you beat me at my favorite video game." He grinned. "But actually, I think it's kind of cool. I'd like to go out with you again."

Emma's mouth dropped open. "You would?"

"Yeah. I really like you."

Or someone who looks a lot like me, Emma thought, smiling.

"I know I didn't say much last time. That was just because I was so surprised. Surprised in a good way, I mean."

"Sam's going to be psyched!" Emma blurted, before she could stop herself.

"Sam?"

"Uh, yeah. She takes a real interest in my personal life. Believe me when I tell you this. She'll be just as glad as I am to hear you had fun on our last date. Maybe even more."

Greg gave her a puzzled look. But Emma hardly noticed. She was too busy imagining the look on Sam's face when she heard the news.

The next day, Sam stood on the sidelines. At least watching the Buzzards' practice was keeping her mind off other stuff. Like the fact that Greg Jacobs wanted a second date! With her! She never would have believed it.

The problem was, Greg expected to pick her up after the Hurricanes game. She and Emma had decided there was only one thing to do: They had to come clean to Greg and hope he'd understand. They were going to tell him tomorrow in school.

But Sam refused to worry about that now. She kept her attention on the Buzzards. In three minutes, she counted twenty-four failed goal attempts. Nobody complained. And no one gave up. Sam had to give the team this much: They did try hard.

They probably thought she was a real creep for ditching them.

She picked up a ball and began to bounce it

from knee to knee. Then she noticed some of her teammates approaching. Even from a distance, she could see the light glinting off Oscar's headgear.

"Hi, Sam."

"Hi, Oscar."

She was about to apologize for bailing. But Oscar hurried on, "We heard about the swap. We want you to know we don't take it personally."

"Right," Jeffrey added. "I mean, we know we aren't the best players in the league. We're sorry. Now that you're back, we'll try not to cramp your style too much."

Sam smiled. She noticed that today, Jeffrey's sunscreen was limited to a white coating on his nose. "Thanks," she said. "It's cool of you guys to say that. Especially when I'm the one who should apologize." She offered Oscar a high five. He missed her hand by a good six inches.

Coach Willard appeared and gave a loud blast on his whistle. "Listen up, team! This is a banner day for the Buzzards. We're welcoming Sam back. And I'm proud to announce a new addition to our coaching staff." He jerked his thumb toward the parking lot.

Sam looked—and gasped. She couldn't believe her eyes.

"Kids," said Willard, "meet our new assistant coach."

Denise Stanton smiled at the group. Her eyes rested finally on Sam.

"Mom?" Sam squeaked.

"That's *Coach Stanton* to you," Denise said. "I changed my seminar. I needed to work out some Family Dynamics of my own." She glanced at Willard. "I'm just going to jump right in, okay?"

Willard waved a hand. "Be my guest!"

Willard stood off to the side. He practiced his golf swing and let Denise do the talking. She told the team that they needed to let go of all their negative energy and visualize a victory.

How can they visualize a victory? Sam wondered. *They've never seen one before.*

"You need to get in touch with your inner goalie," Denise told Jeffrey. Then she turned to Oscar. "Celebrate your uniqueness!" she advised.

Oscar looked confused.

Sam rubbed her temples. "Great," she muttered. "Psycho-soccer. Can it get any worse?"

"Rejoice in the power of individuality! Let your positive vibe overtake your fear of failure and rid you of self-destructive tendencies."

All eyes turned to Sam for help. She sighed. "Let

me put this in terms you guys will understand," she said. "Just go out there, and try not to get hurt."

The Buzzards stumbled out to the field and began a scrimmage.

"Nicky!" Denise called to the kid in the football helmet. "Pass the ball to Sam!"

"I don't know how!" Nicky hollered back.

"Hmm." Denise tapped her chin. "And how does that make you feel?"

Sam wanted to scream.

Finally, Coach Stanton, PhD., called the players back to the sidelines. "I think we need to change our strategy," she said. She reached out and drummed her fingers on Nicky's helmet. "It's time to rethink our strengths and use what we've got."

Oscar's headgear caught the afternoon sunlight. Sam held up a hand to shield her eyes. Then she stared—as she saw the grin on her mother's face.

"Hmmm. Maybe we've got more than we think," Denise said.

Every Buzzard head turned to look at Sam. She knew they were expecting her to translate again.

But all Sam could do was shrug. She didn't have the slightest idea what her mom had in mind.

She knew only one thing for certain.

Her life was over!

CHAPTER THIRTEEN

Sam and Emma stood at the end of the school corridor. They were watching Greg at his locker.

"Are you sure we have to tell him?" Sam asked.

"Positive," Emma said.

Sam drew a deep breath. Then she approached Greg. Emma was right behind her. He turned and smiled at them.

"Hi, Emma. Hi, Sam."

"Um, we have something to tell you," Emma began.

Greg's eyes darted from twin to twin. "We?"

"It's like this…" Sam began. Then, she closed her eyes tightly. And blurted out the whole horrible truth.

The next thing Sam knew, she and Emma were chasing Greg down the hall and out the doors.

"Wait!" Emma called. "Please!"

"Why should I?" Greg turned to face them. The look on his face was part angry, part hurt. "I asked out Emma, and got Sam as a substitute. You guys got a good laugh at my expense."

"No, we didn't," Sam insisted. "We never meant it to be a joke. We only did it because—because I hoped if you had a chance to get to know me, you might...like me."

Greg paused. "Well, that's the rotten thing about this, Sam. I really did like you."

Sam gulped. "Did? Is that past tense?"

Greg didn't answer.

She forced herself to ask another question. "What about Saturday?"

"As far as I'm concerned, you can both stay home." With that, Greg took off down the steps and across the parking lot.

Sam stared after him. "Now what?" she asked.

Emma sighed. "Now we go home and hope he has a change of heart."

Silently, the girls headed toward the playing fields. Sam felt as though she had ice cubes in her stomach. Her throat was tight and her eyes stung.

She found an abandoned soccer ball in the grass. Absently, she began to dribble it.

"Why does it have to hurt so much?" she asked. She looked up at Emma, who was standing in front of the goal.

"I don't know," Emma said gently.

"If only this romance junk came as easy to me as sports," Sam grumbled.

"If only this sports junk came as easy to me as romance," Emma sighed.

Almost without thinking, Sam sent the ball screaming toward the goal.

And almost without thinking, Emma raised her hands and whacked it away from the net.

Sam blinked.

Emma blinked.

"Did that just happen?" asked Sam. She scooped up the ball.

"It must have been a fluke," Emma said.

Sam suddenly dropped the ball and kicked it toward the goal.

Emma made another miraculous grab.

"Whoa!" Sam said.

"Yeah," Emma breathed. *"Whoa."*

"You're a natural, Em! We've got to tell Dad. He can put you in as goalie!"

Emma's eyes widened. She shook her head hard. "Richie is the goalie. He'd throw a fit if Dad replaced him with me. Besides, I wouldn't want to take his place."

Sam cracked a grin. "Is that because you want to play fair? Or is it because you still think he's cute?"

Before Emma could answer, Sam sent the ball flying toward the goal.

Emma reached out and ended its flight with one hand. She grinned back at her sister. "Both," she admitted.

On Saturday, the Buzzards, under the direction of Coach Stanton, won their first game ever.

Much of the credit went to Oscar's "brilliant" defense. His job was to position himself by the goal. Then he used his shiny metal headgear to blind the opposing goalie. Nicky celebrated his own uniqueness too. He bounced ball after ball off his helmet— and into the net past the squinting goal tender.

Jeffrey's sunblock came in handy as well. As luck would have it, the other team's leading scorer was allergic to coconut. Every time the kid got close to the goal, he'd break into a sneezing fit. Sam was always around to steal the ball and pass it to safety.

"Are you sure we're not playing dirty?" Sam asked her mother after the game. They were on their way to catch the last few minutes of the Hurricanes' game.

"I wouldn't call it dirty," Denise said. "I prefer to look at it in psychological terms. Let's say the Buzzards are turning their personal liabilities into vehicles for success."

"Let's just say," said Sam, giggling, "that the Buzzards are cleaning up—big time!"

Her mom smiled. "Works for me."

With thirty seconds left in the game, the Hurricanes and the Bulls were tied, 2-2.

"You all know how I feel about a tie," Jerry yelled. "Don't you?"

The exhausted Hurricanes nodded.

"But Coach," Richie said, "that Number 23 for the Bulls is a defense machine! You can't get by him. The kid's a monster!"

"He's not a monster," said Emma. She glanced over her shoulder and waved her fingers at Number 23. "Actually, he's kind of sweet. Every time I get near him, he smiles at me."

Jerry scowled as the monster smiled stupidly and returned Emma's wave. He was about to scold her. Then an idea struck him.

"Okay, guys, here's the play," he said quickly. "Danny, you pass the ball to Andy, who'll be coming down the middle. Andy, you lay the ball off on Fred. He's going to dribble past Emma. Very important, Fred, *dribble past Emma.*"

Fred looked puzzled, but nodded.

"What am I going to do, Dad?" asked Emma.

Grinning, Jerry draped his arm around Emma. Then he bent close to her ear, and whispered his explanation.

The play went off as planned. Danny to Andy, Andy to Fred. Number 23, however, saw it coming. He went charging toward Fred to steal.

But before he could reach Fred, Emma stepped into his path—and gave him a world-class hair toss.

It stopped Number 23 in his tracks.

"Hi," Emma said in a flirty voice. "You don't mind if I just stand here and stop you from messing up this play, do you?"

Dazed, 23 shook his head. He never took his eyes off Emma. Only the sound of the crowd cheering Fred's goal broke 23 out of his trance. But by then it was too late. The Hurricanes had a victory!

On the sidelines, Sam gave Emma a high five. "Nice work out there. In basketball, that's called a screen."

"In romance, it's called bringing them to their knees." Emma giggled. "Hey, how was your game?"

"We won!" Denise answered.

"Wow!" Jerry blurted out. "That's unbelievable!"

Sam didn't miss the annoyed look her mom gave

her dad. "Yeah," she said quickly. "Mom came up with some awesome strategy. Not exactly textbook soccer. But it got the job done."

"So you turned out to be a heck of an assistant coach, huh?" Smiling, Jerry leaned over to give his wife a kiss.

Denise dodged him. "Try *head* coach," she said. "Willard promoted me this afternoon." She gave him a tight grin. "And you know what? The Buzzards are going to make roadkill out of the Hurricanes when we play you." She turned and headed for her car.

"Looks like someone's gotten in touch with her inner competitor," Jerry snapped. Then he took off for his van.

The girls looked at one another.

"I thought they were supposed to be the grown-ups," Sam said.

Emma shook her head. She ran after their dad. Sam hurried to catch up with their mom.

Correction. With Head Coach Stanton.

CHAPTER FOURTEEN

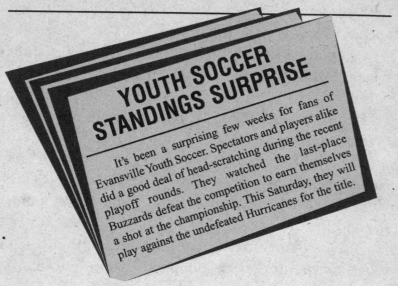

YOUTH SOCCER STANDINGS SURPRISE

It's been a surprising few weeks for fans of Evansville Youth Soccer. Spectators and players alike did a good deal of head-scratching during the recent playoff rounds. They watched the last-place Buzzards defeat the competition to earn themselves a shot at the championship. This Saturday, they will play against the undefeated Hurricanes for the title.

On the morning of the big game, Sam and Emma stood together on the field. They gazed in awe at the crowded bleachers. It was the biggest turnout in Evansville Youth Soccer history.

"You'd think they'd never seen the Buzzards in the finals before," grumbled Sam.

Emma gave her a friendly elbow to the ribs. "They haven't!"

They wished each other luck. Then they went to join their teams.

Sam found her mother putting a last-minute

polish on Oscar's braces.

"What was it you used to say about Dad?" Sam teased. "He was overcompetitive?"

Denise gave her a warning look.

Sam laughed.

On the other side of the field, Jerry was giving the Hurricanes a pep talk. He turned to Emma. "Have you got everything you need?" he asked. "Lip gloss, hair spray, perfume?"

"Got it all, Dad." Emma held up her gym bag. "All my soccer essentials."

"Good girl."

The game began.

Unfortunately for the Hurricanes, though, Emma's flirty defense didn't seem to be working this time. She winked at Oscar, waved to Jeffrey, and blew a kiss to Nicky. But they didn't even notice.

Finally Jerry called a time-out, and Emma came back to the bench. "You were like kryptonite to the players on those other teams," Jerry moaned. "Why not the Buzzards?"

The Buzzards weren't having much luck, either. Every time Sam passed Nicky the ball, his helmet sent it out of bounds and into the bleachers. Once it even sailed clear across the parking lot.

Then, halfway through the first period, clouds rolled in. They blocked the sun. Oscar's blinding headgear was useless.

The game wore on. It seemed as if no one on either team could find the goal. Finally, there were only two minutes left on the clock. Neither team had scored.

Sam had the ball. She shot it toward the goal. Richie lunged, punching it away from the net. It was a great save. But he came down hard on his right shoulder.

Frantic, Jerry called a time-out. He hurried to where Richie lay in the grass. Dave, carrying an ice pack, was close at his heels.

"Are you okay?" Jerry asked. He felt the goalie's shoulder bone.

"It hurts pretty bad, Coach," said Richie. "But I can still play." He tried to move his arm and winced.

Jerry looked at the beads of sweat on Richie's forehead. He sighed. "No way, son. I appreciate your dedication. But I can't let you play in pain."

Dave helped Richie back to the bench. The crowd ooohed and aaahed in sympathy. Jerry stood on the field. Who could he could put in as goalie?

"Dad?"

He turned to see Sam standing beside him.

"Dad, you've got to let Emma tend goal. Believe me, she's a natural."

Jerry scowled. "Is this one of your mom's tricks?"

"No, Dad. I swear! Emma and I were practicing the other day. She blocked everything. She's dying for the chance to have you see how good she is."

Jerry chewed his lip. Then he glanced at the scoreboard.

"Come on, Dad. Can't you just drop the winning thing? Just this once? So what if you lose? Think of how much this will mean to Emma."

The twins' father swallowed hard. He looked over his shoulder toward Emma. She was sitting on the bench. Putting her in could mean the difference between winning and losing.

Then he remembered the day they worked together. He smiled. She had tried so hard. She'd wanted to make him proud.

Suddenly, Jerry realized how very proud he was.

"I'll do it!" he said. "I'll give her a chance. She deserves it."

He turned and marched back to the bench. "Emma, come on, kiddo. You're taking Richie's place at goal."

"Me?" Emma gulped. "Are you sure? Isn't that a really important position?"

Jerry smiled and smoothed her hair. "Em, president of the United States is an important position. Goalie is just part of the game. Now go out there and do your best."

The ref's whistle blew. Emma gave her father a hug. Then she hurried to the goal.

"I'm not going to go easy on you," Sam warned Emma with a grin.

"You won't have to," Emma called back, laughing with excitement.

Sam gave her sister a thumbs-up. Then the game started again.

For the final minute, it looked more like a game of keep-away than soccer. The ball bounced from team to team. No one was able to hold on to it long enough to score.

At last, Oscar managed to pass to Sam. She had a clear shot at the goal. The only thing in her way was...her sister.

The twins faced each other. Emma dug in as Sam began her breakaway. She angled for position. Emma crouched low, centering her weight.

Sam stopped, hovering over the ball.

Emma focused on the movement. She held out

both hands, palms face-out. She was actually grinding her teeth!

Sam swung back her foot with all her strength. Then she slammed it hard against the ball.

Emma took a fast side-step. She raised her arms.

The ball went rocketing toward the upper right-hand corner of the net.

So did Emma. She dove, reaching one hand out fast.

For a moment, the ball seemed to hang in the air.

Then...Emma's fingertips grazed the ball. It flew up and over the goal—just as the final buzzer sounded.

The game was over—and the score was 0-0!

Sam was the first one into the goal to hug Emma. Jerry was close behind. He lifted Emma and spun her around.

"Thanks for giving me a chance, Dad," Emma whispered.

Jerry placed her down and looked her in the eye. "Actually, *you* gave *me* a chance, Emma. A chance to become a better Dad." He smiled. "So I was thinking. Maybe tomorrow, you and I could go to the mall or something."

At that moment, Denise appeared. She threw her arms around Emma, then around Sam. Then, to the twins' relief, she hugged their dad.

"Forget the Buzzards and the Hurricanes," she said. "Let's hear it for Team Stanton!"

Sam and Emma cheered wildly.

At the closing ceremony, Mr. Eldridge stood and made a special announcement. It was the first time in the league's history that there was a tie for the championship. "So," Mr. Eldridge said, "we'll be engraving *two* championship plaques this season. One for the Hurricanes, and one for the Buzzards."

After the clapping and cheering was over, the crowd began to leave. The players gathered up their things.

"Uh-oh," Emma said to Sam. "Look who's here."

Sam looked up. Her heart turned over. Greg was waiting on the bottom bleacher.

She lifted her gym bag onto her shoulder. "I guess we should go see what he wants," she said. Nervously, she headed for the stands. Emma was right behind her.

"Hi, Greg," Sam said.

"Hi, Sam. Good game." He turned to Emma. "You, too."

"Thanks."

He looked down. "Look, uh—I'm sorry about the other day. About how I acted when you told me what you did. It's just that...well, I was kind of confused. But I think I figured it out." He looked up at Sam and gave her a smile.

Sam felt a tingle in her stomach. "Really?"

Greg nodded. "Are you busy tonight, Sam?"

Grinning, Emma gave her twin a little push in Greg's direction. "She is now!"

Greg took Sam's gym bag. The three of them began to walk toward the parking lot.

"Hey, wait up!" came a voice from behind them.

They all turned to see Richie trying to catch up to them. His sore shoulder was obviously making it hard for him to carry his gear.

Sam watched as her sister hurried toward Richie and took the heavy bag from him.

"Thanks," Richie said. His cheeks turned red.

"No problem."

He glanced at the ground. His cheeks turned even redder. "I just wanted to tell you, Emma. That was a great save."

Emma shrugged. "It was okay, I guess."

Richie turned back to Emma. "So, um, are you doing anything tonight?"

Sam gave a shocked Emma a nudge toward Richie. "She is now!"

Laughing, the four of them made plans for a double date at Slappy's at seven—sharp. Then Emma helped Richie carry his gym bag to where his dad's car was waiting.

Greg turned to Sam. "I missed the game. So what was the score, anyway?"

"It was a tie," Sam told him.

Greg took her hand in his. "So nobody won?" he asked.

Sam glanced back at Emma and Richie. Then at her mom and dad, who were holding hands as they chatted with Willard.

"Actually," she said, "This time, everybody won!"